KU-385-492

Lilac Peabody

and
Sam Sparks

Also by Annie Dalton:

The *Angels Unlimited* series

Winging It
Losing the Plot
Flying High
Calling the Shots
Fogging Over
Fighting Fit
Making Waves

Lilac peabody

and
Sam Sparks

ANNIE DALTON

Illustrated by Griff

An imprint of HarperCollinsPublishers

PERTH AND KINROSS LIBRARIES

.344681

To Sophie and Izzie
with love

First published in Great Britain by HarperCollins*Children'sBooks* in 2004
HarperCollins*Children'sBooks* is an imprint of HarperCollins*Publishers* Ltd
77-85 Fulham Palace Road, Hammersmith, London W6 8JB

The HarperCollins website address is www.harpercollins.co.uk

1 3 5 7 9 8 6 4 2

Text copyright © Annie Dalton 2004
Illustrations © Andrew Griffin 2004

ISBN 0 00 713771 0

The author asserts her moral right
to be identified as the author of the work.

Printed and bound in England by
Clays Ltd, St Ives plc

Conditions of Sale
This book is sold subject to the condition
that it shall not, by way of trade or otherwise,
be lent, re-sold, hired out or otherwise circulated
without the publisher's prior consent in any form,
binding or cover other than that in which it is
published and without a similar condition
including this condition being imposed on the
subsequent purchaser.

1.

Extraterrestrial Busybody

This story starts in a big white rental van one stuffy grey afternoon.

The van contains everything my mum and I own in the world, which isn't that much, but sounds like World War Two when it's all banging about in the back.

We're just going round the same roundabout for the third, maybe the fourth time. I'm saying, "Mum the exit's back there!" and, "Mum, what are you *doing*? That guy just flashed his lights at us!"

"Hey Sparkster, relax," Mum says. "That's why roundabouts were invented. So people could take their time to work out which exit is the right one!"

It's useless arguing when Mum gets like this. She'll go round another three times, just to make her point, and I'm already feeling as sick as a P. I. G. from that burger at the service station.

So I do what I always do. I pretend this isn't happening. I pretend I'm watching a movie about a boy with a ditzy single mum who thinks getting lost in a new town is hilarious; a mum who makes her son move house so often you'd be forgiven for thinking she was on the run.

OK, that's too harsh. Mum is

a bit scary when she gets

behind a wheel, but no way could she ever be a menace to society. She'd never knowingly upset anybody. Well, yeah, me. But to be fair, she doesn't actually *know* she's upsetting me. Every time she says, "Hey, Sparkster, I've got this great new job in

this great new place, it's a chance for a better life,"
I just go, "Fine! Go for it, Mum. Whatever!"

"Tell her the truth, Sam," Lilac Peabody keeps saying. "Tell her it's not fine to keep on uprooting you. You were just settling into that school. You were just starting to get friends."

I shrug. "Grown-ups don't listen to kids, everyone knows that."

"How can she listen when you keep everything all bottled up inside?" Lilac complains. "Your mother's not a mind-reader, unlike me."

And she gives me one of her secretive smiles.

Bums! I was going to work up to telling you about Lilac Peabody, but now she's just jumped into the story, feet first, so I'd better explain.

Actually, it's easier if I show you.

Rewind back to the beginning of this story. Same stuffy afternoon. Same big white rental van. *Exactly* the same roundabout. Mum and I are now making our fifth or sixth circuit. That's me, the boy with the mad Afro. Mum got so stressed with packing up for the move, she totally forgot to take me to the barber's.

Now look closely at the front seat, between me and Mum. Closer. Just a little bit closer. See that blurry golden glow? No? Keep looking. Bull's-eye!!

No, you're not imagining things. That's her. That's Lilac Peabody. For some reason I'm the only one who sees her, which is just as well. I don't think Mum would be too thrilled to be rubbing shoulders with a little glow-in-the-dark alien.

Even leaving out the glow, Lilac looks completely different from humans. For one thing, she has wings. Also, her skin has a very faint blue-green shimmer. Her eyes are different too. Larger and wiser than human eyes.

But I've learned one thing about Lilac Peabody over the past few months. She only ever shows up when there's a problem. And the fact is, we've *got* a problem. We've been going round this roundabout so long the sun is starting to set. But the ditzy mum in my movie won't admit anything's wrong. She's actually singing to herself as if she's having the time of her life.

"Life is not a movie, Sam," Lilac whispers. "This is really happening. Your mum's scared. Look at her eyes."

I sneak a look at my mother and I get a sick feeling inside that is more than just the dodgy burger. She looks glazed with terror, like a wild rabbit in the glare of car headlights.

My one remaining parent and she's lost the plot.

"Your mum's scared she's done something stupid," Lilac says into my ear. "Taking this job, going to another town."

"It is stupid," I hiss angrily. "It was a bad idea from Day One."

"Doesn't matter. It's happening, and it's all going to work out. But right now your mum needs your help."

I stare at her as if she's nuts. "What can I do? I'm only nine years old! In my galaxy that means I'm not allowed to drive. I can't even reach the pedals."

"You don't need to drive, Sam. All you've got to do is crack a joke."

"I'm not in a joking mood, OK?" That's an understatement. If we go round this roundabout one more time, I'm probably going to throw up.

Lilac Peabody narrows her eyes. "Remember what I told you about cosmic timing?"

I nod queasily.

"Good," she says in a firm voice. "So crack a good joke and do it for real."

"They should call you Lilac Busybody," I mutter.

She laughs. "That's funny! Now let me see you use that smart tongue to help your mum."

That's another thing I've learned about Lilac Peabody. She can be REALLY persistent when she wants to be.

She just won't let up until you agree she's got a point.

So I swallow hard and I say, "Hey Mum, I'm going to give you two choices. Option one, we forget about the house and just camp on the roundabout like hippies, maybe breed rare chickens. Or, option two, you drive me past my new school, so I can actually see where it is before it gets dark."

I feel a funny kind of "click" inside me and, like magic, Mum's eyes come back into focus. She

splutters with laughter. It's almost like she's been floundering underwater and my joke made her shoot back up to the surface.

"Sparkster, you're something else," she marvels. "Rare chickens! We could be the famous roundabout hippies. We could sell cream teas."

"Ahem! Herbal teas, excuse me! And maybe apple juice for the kids."

"We'd be a tourist attraction," she giggles.

"People would come for miles. Plus you notice I already have the mad hippie hair."

Mum sighs, "Sorry, Sam."

"That's OK," I say. "I can go to the barber's after school on Monday."

"Not about the hair. I was panicking back there."

"Everyone panics sometimes," I tell her. "Don't worry about it. Look, the exit's just coming up on your left."

Mum indicates left and turns off so smoothly you'd never think she'd had a moment's doubt. It's such a good feeling to be travelling in

straight lines that I keep up a stream of silly roundabout jokes out of pure relief.

I don't even notice when Lilac quietly disappears.

My mother drives past my new school, which looks like a million other schools, and after that we go straight to our new home, which is a sad dump like every other place we've lived since Dad left. But none of these things matter just now, because surprisingly Mum and I are suddenly having a great time.

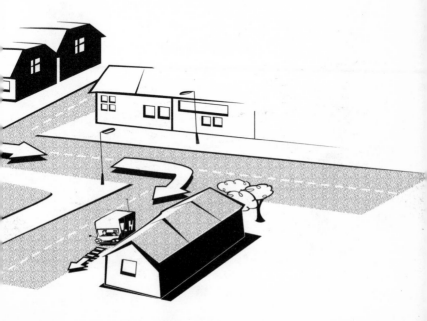

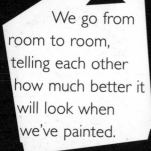

We go from room to room, telling each other how much better it will look when we've painted.

And OK, it doesn't have much of a garden, but there's a big park at the back that is almost as good.

Mum and I unpack just the stuff we'll need for the night, and set up a base camp with blankets and mattresses by the gas fire. Mum unpacks the picnic she made for us before we left. It tastes a bit interesting after being in a van for four hours. Then I brush my teeth and settle down for the night.

"We'll get your room sorted out tomorrow," Mum says. "Tonight we'll just be roundabout hippies."

"Peace and love man," I say. "And don't forget to shut the door when you chat to Auntie Jasmine on the phone."

"Who says I'm going to chat to Jasmine, Mister Smarty-pants?"

I give her my look.

She grins. "You are just too clever for your own good, Sam Sparks!"

Mum goes off into the hall with her mobile and, like always, she forgets to close the door so I have to hear her talking about me, which I hate. "I just hope this works out. Sam is such a great kid. He deserves the best."

I lie looking at the blue and orange gas flames and I make three wishes.

I wish that this time we'll stay in the same town for longer than six months. I wish that this time I get the chance to make some real human mates. And I wish something that I know, even as I'm wishing, is totally impossible.

I wish that at the end of next week, when it's my birthday, I can have a real birthday party with real friends, the way I've always dreamed. I don't wish about my dad any more because like Mum says, some doors are closed.

Just before I go to sleep I hear a *fitzz* like a sparkler being lit, and she's back, sitting cross-legged by the fire.

"What you been up to, Peebs?" I say sleepily.

"A spot of beachcombing," she says.

"Fibber! There's no beach near here."

Lilac Peabody gives me her secretive smile.

"Did I say it was near here?"

I raise myself up on one elbow. "Is that what it says on your passport? Cosmic Beachcomber?"

She chuckles. "That's nice, Sam. I think I'll put that after Extraterrestrial Busybody!"

It bothers me sometimes that I don't actually know who or what Lilac Peabody is. The first time she showed up, after my dad walked out,

I just assumed she was a visitor from another planet, but I don't know this for sure. I'm not even a hundred per cent certain that Lilac Peabody is her real name.

I watch her in the fire light.

As usual she's wearing an assortment of weird glittery clothes which look like things you'd find in a kid's dressing-up box.

They make her look as if she's on her way to some wild extraterrestrial carnival. I've noticed that no matter what's happening, Lilac Peabody always seems to be having a great time.

"I just want a party, Peebs," I tell her. "A real party, just once."

"Your mum made invitations," she says. "You could take them in on Monday."

"I'll be the new boy. The other kids will look through me like I'm not even there."

"You can still take them," suggests Lilac. "You could be the really weird new boy who hands out birthday invitations on his first day at school!"

"Maybe," I say, meaning maybe not.

Lilac starts to hum.

"What else is on your passport, Peebs?" I ask drowsily. "Extraterrestrial Busybody, Cosmic Beachcomber, and what else?"

She doesn't answer. For a few minutes the only sounds are the soothing popping sounds of the gas fire mingling with Lilac Peabody's thoughtful humming.

Just as I'm finally drifting off I hear her say softly:

"Intergalactic Party Planner."

2.
Poodle Head

Listen! I've been the new kid so often, I could write *The New Kids' Rule Book*.

(Rule Number One: Trust no one.)

So when everyone ignores me on my first day,

I'm disappointed but not all that surprised. I'm a boy, you see. When a new girl arrives at your school, all the girls compete like crazy to see who's going to be her special best friend. Boys wait to see if you'll turn out to be cool enough to bother with. Meanwhile, they act as if you're a speck of dog dirt that came in on someone's shoe.

This probationary period can last a couple of days, or several weeks. There's no way of knowing. Of course, while I'm waiting to pass the Cool Test, I'm also checking the other kids out.

At lunch time, Lilac Peabody and I meet up in a quiet corner of the playground and I tell her that I've already figured out who to avoid.

"Honey Hope," she sighs.

"How did you know?"

She taps her nose. "Special Powers, remember."

"That girl just has a grudge against the whole world," I tell her.

"She certainly has a grudge against Bella Bright."

Too right. Honey is on Bella's case all day long: making fun of her clothes, her hair, the way she talks.

In the cafeteria she rips the lid off Bella's lunch box and says, "Peeyoo! What's this stinky stuff?" and waves two slices of very strange-looking garlic sausage.

(Rule Number Two: Never have anything *unusual* in your lunch box. It'll save you loads of grief.)

There's nothing wrong with Bella Bright that I can see. Yet it isn't just Honey who acts as if Bella's something whiffy that just blew in from the council tip. Everyone in my class

treats her the same way. At break time she walks around by herself, with her shoulders hunched around her ears. Even Miss Mays, our teacher, ignores her. I can't believe it!

Even when Bella is shyly waving her hand because she knows the answer!

I think Lilac Peabody's mind-reading skills might be rubbing off, because I suddenly know what's going on. They're scared. They don't dare be nice to Bella. They daren't even risk being polite, just in case they're next on Honey's hit list.

The only kid who stands up to Honey is Charlie. Correction, he doesn't exactly stand up to her; that's not Charlie's style. But during the garlic-sausage incident, he's doing everything he can to distract Honey: clowning around, making out she's a scary superhero who gets her super-strength from some special honey made by special bees back on her home planet.

He gets away with it too. Charlie Chase is one of those crazy kids. You only have to look at him to see that. He's crazy, but he isn't mean. When Honey comes out with her poisonous comments, you can see the teacher tensing up. But when Charlie makes one of his mad cracks, Miss Mays can't help laughing. She tries to tell him off but she has a naughty glint in her eye, as if she's saying, "What are we going to do with this boy?!"

Charlie is the kind of boy I've always dreamed of being best mates with, but he's so popular it's depressing. Everyone in our class wants to be his friend. No way does he need me hanging around. He's the school superstar whereas I'm

just average. I don't have the latest clothes. I don't even own a computer, and anyway, in six months' time Mum and I will probably be moving on.

By home time I am convinced that no one at my new school will ever like me. Lilac Peabody makes out it's the easiest thing in the world to go up to my new classmates and hand out party invitations. But what's the point? I'm lower than a germ at this school, and just as invisible. Even the class bully doesn't notice me.

Mum meets me after school. I'm stressed from my day and she's stressed from hers. We walk all the way home, snapping and stressing, before we remember I was meant to be going to the barber's.

Lilac Peabody has been tactfully keeping her distance, but when I'm finally alone in my room, I hear that soft sparkler *fitzz*, and there she is, sitting on my chest of drawers in a halo of golden light. "You didn't give out the invitations,"

she says in an accusing voice.

I must look really upset because she says quickly, "Never mind there's always tomorrow."

"Yeah," I say bravely. "Tomorrow will be better."

It isn't. It's much *much* worse.

Next morning, while our teacher is calling the register, Honey Hope sits with her eyes half closed, drumming her fingers, tick, tick, tick, like a time bomb getting ready to go off.

My name is last to be called.

"Sam Sparks," says Miss May.

Like an evil mummy in a movie, Honey's eyes fly open.

"Sam Sparks," she repeats in a jeering voice. "That's you, is it, Poodle Head?"

(Rule Number Three: Get your hair cut *before* you start school.)

Everyone shrieks with laughter, mixed with major relief that Honey didn't pick on them. All day kids smirk at me, and whisper, "Poodle Head," from behind their hands.

That night I drag Mum to the local barber's where I get the most drastic haircut in history. But it's too late. Honey's spiteful nickname has stuck like superglue. When I go into the playground next morning, all I hear is, "Poodle Head, Poodle Head." Even cheeky little infants are calling me Poodle Head!

I notice Lilac Peabody watching from a perch on the playground wall. She's waving frantically.

I see her mouth, "Don't forget the invitations."

I open my bag and take them out. Turning my back on her, I dump the invitations in the nearest litter bin.

This has to be the worst day of my life. I thought I'd hated it when I was invisible, but now I see how lucky I was. Now I only have to cough for Honey Hope to make some vicious remark.

When I get home that night, Lilac firmly hands me back my invitations.

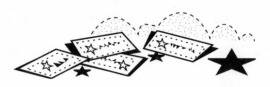

"It's going to be all right," she tells me. "Cosmic timing, remember?"

I tell her to stuff her cosmic timing. I tell her that a stupid little space alien can't possibly understand how horrible it is being at school on Earth when no one wants to be your friend. Next day I dump the party invitations back in the bin.

It goes on like this. Me throwing the invitations away, Lilac stubbornly rescuing them and giving them back. Until finally it's the day before my birthday.

Despite the fact that I keep binning my invitations, I've been secretly hoping Lilac Peabody will come up with some whizzy extraterrestrial solution to my popularity problem, and I'll get my birthday party after all.

Now, suddenly, I realise this isn't going to happen. Not only have I *not* passed the Cool Test, I am now joint class victim with Bella Bright.

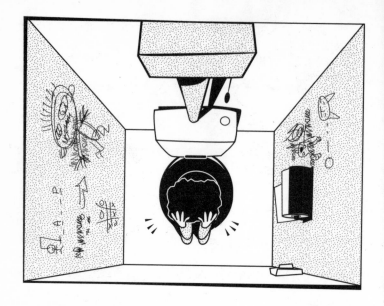

I've never done anything to Honey Hope, yet it feels like she's on a personal mission to destroy me. By lunch time I'm in bits. I can't see an end to it, and I absolutely can't take any more. I run into the boys' toilets, shut myself in a cubicle and cry like a girl.

After about fifteen minutes I pull myself together and wash my face.

As I come out, a small voice says, "Hi."

It's Bella, nervously chewing the end of her plait.

"Hi," I say in a gruff voice, hoping I don't look too damp and blubbery.

"I just wanted to say sorry. I know what it's like when Honey has it in for you." Bella gives a shy smile. "To be honest, it's nice for me she's torturing someone else for a change."

Someone at this school is finally talking to me. But the sad girl everybody picks on is not exactly my first choice for a friend. However anything's better than spending yet another lunch hour skulking around by myself, so we find

an empty table by the window and eat our sandwiches together.

Despite being so shy, Bella's easy to talk to. I find myself telling her about my nutty mum and how she insists on calling me Sparkster, like some kid gangster, and how I'm sick to death of moving from place to place and never having any real mates. To my surprise, Bella says she used to be really good buddies with Honey. Then they started in a new class and suddenly

Bella was Enemy Number One. To this day she doesn't know what she did wrong.

I hear a familiar fizzing sound.

"Invite Bella to your party," Lilac Peabody whispers in my ear.

"Get lost Peebs," I say out of the corner of my mouth.

No way am I going to have some sad victims' tea party with Bella!

That night, I go to say goodnight to Mum. She's busy chatting to Auntie Jasmine, so I hover in the doorway waiting for her to get off the phone. Mum hasn't noticed I'm there.

To my horror, I see she's flicking through our big road atlas. I hear her say something about London.

We've just got here and Mum's thinking about moving already.

3.
Sam Sparks's Special Powers

I rush up to my bedroom and throw myself on the bed. I might be miserable at my new school, but the thought of moving to *another* strange school makes me frantic.

There's a soft *fitzz* and my room lights up with a starry glow.

"It's going to be all right," says Lilac Peabody.

"Will you stop saying that?" I yell.

"It's true," she says calmly.

"You tell me all this stuff, but you won't help. If you've got all these amazing extraterrestrial Special Powers, why won't you help?"

My voice cracks with misery. Lilac Peabody pats my shoulder. It's the first time she's actually touched me. It feels slightly fizzy, like faint electric shocks.

"You're the one with the powers," she says. "Even your name is special."

"Yeah, Poodle Head is a *really* special name," I say bitterly.

"I'm talking about your real name. Sam Sparks. It sounds like a boy who makes things happen."

"It's just a name and I don't have any Special Powers," I tell her.

"Remember when your mum panicked at the roundabout," Lilac says, "and I said you just had to tell a joke and everything would be OK. Was I wrong?"

"No," I mumble.

"When you told the joke did you feel something change?"

"No," I say. "Yes… I don't know."

"You didn't feel a little tiny click like a train switching tracks?"

"Maybe," I admit grudgingly.

"That's the feeling you get when something bad turns into something good."

I fold my arms across my chest. "Thanks for the inside info. If anything good ever happens to me again, I'll remember that."

"It *will*, Sam, I promise. It's all a matter of—"

"Cosmic timing," I say wearily. "Yeah, yeah."

"You can stay in this town," Lilac says in an earnest voice. "You can stay at this school and make great friends. All you have to do is start the ball rolling."

I suddenly see where this is going.

"Stop right there, Peebs," I say. "Because it isn't going to work. You think you're going to keep on at me with your little cosmic cracker mottos until I cave in and invite Bella Bright to my party. Well save your breath, I'm not doing it."

With a quick flouncing movement, Lilac turns her back. I hear her say something under her

breath. I don't quite catch it, but I'm almost certain she said, "roundabout".

She keeps up the pressure for HOURS. When she isn't muttering "roundabout", she's humming a little extraterrestrial tune. Not the dreamy peaceful tune, a really weird one that sets your teeth on edge like you would not believe. There's a genuine danger I'll lose all my tooth enamel so I finally cave in. I promise to invite Bella. But I don't have to be happy about it.

"Great party this is going to be," I sulk. "The two school losers playing Pin the Tail on the Donkey."

Lilac Peabody is all smiles now she's got her own way. "You're not a loser, Sam Sparks," she beams. "And nor is Bella. You are two great kids whose luck is just about to change."

I have to laugh. Lilac Peabody is really something else. Nothing ever seems to get her down.

"Have you got Positive Thinker on your passport too, Peebs?" I tease her.

Maybe positive thinking really does work. Maybe positive thoughts actually hang in the air, like that nice scent Mum wears. Because when I wake up next morning, my room feels all fizzy and happy for no reason. Plus there's always a special feeling, isn't there, when it's your birthday? A kind of birthday zing.

Yeah, well, this year my birthday zing lasts all of five minutes.

When I go downstairs to find Mum – and get my presents – she's nowhere to be seen. I'm all alone in the house.

I'm so shocked I can't even be mad. I absolutely can't believe my mother has just gone off on my birthday without telling me! She hasn't even left me a birthday card, just a bright blue balloon bobbing about on the kitchen ceiling, with a glittery silver tag attached. There's something written on it in Mum's handwriting.

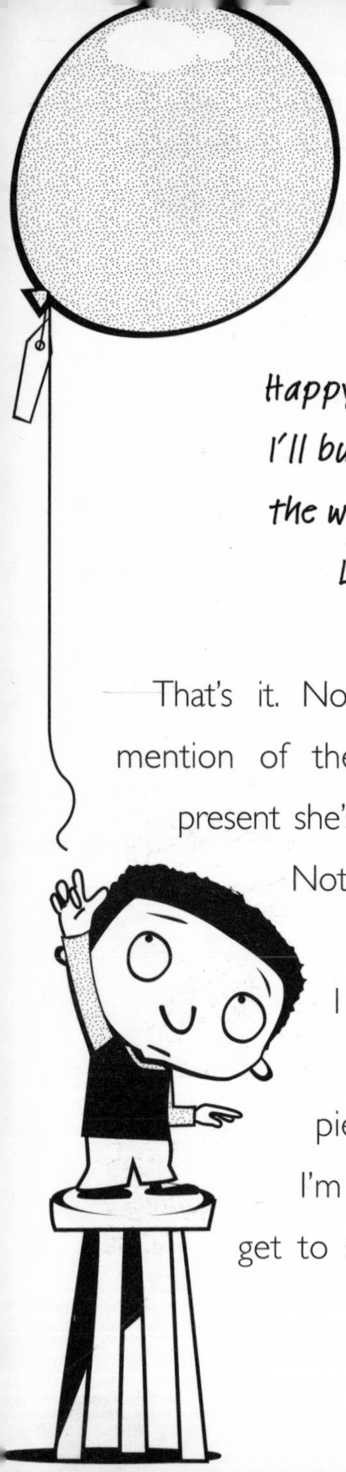

I climb up on a stool, capture the balloon, and untie the tag. It says:

Happy birthday Sparkster!
I'll buy the party food on
the way home.
Love Mum.

That's it. No explanation, no apology. No mention of the humungously cool birthday present she's got stashed away somewhere. Nothing.

"Happy birthday Sparkster," I mutter. "Yeah right!"

And I rip the tag into little pieces.

I'm so miserable by the time I get to school that I totally forget my promise to Lilac Peabody. As we're lining up to go into class, I see a familiar shimmery figure waving wildly.

"OK, OK," I mutter. "I've got the message."

I sidle up to Bella.

"It's my birthday today," I say without enthusiasm. "Will you come to my party?"

And I shove one of my battered invitations into her hand.

For a moment Bella looks as if she's going to burst into tears. When she can speak, she says, "Do you mean it, Sam? You really want me to come? I mean *really*?"

"I said so didn't I?" I growl.

I feel like such a jerk. I gave Bella this half-hearted invitation and she's so grateful it's embarrassing – when I wouldn't even be *asking* her if it wasn't for Lilac Peabody.

"Don't expect too much," I add gruffly. "It'll just be cake and sandwiches."

"No, it's going to be brilliant. I'll bring a surprise, I promise!" Her face is shining with excitement.

Great, she's going to get me that game of Pin the Tail on the Donkey.

"That'll be nice," I say bravely.

Lilac Peabody gives me a delighted thumbs-up from the school wall. Like, "Ooh,

Sam, everything is going to be OK from now on."

I don't believe this for a moment, but I'm happy to see the sparkle in Bella's eyes. I can almost see what she might have been like, before she started looking over her shoulder constantly, waiting for Honey to pounce.

I'm so happy that at lunch time I do something really stupid. I try to join in a football game with Charlie and the other cool boys.

(Rule Number Four: Never try to join in until you're actually invited.)

As I'm running after the ball, Charlie trips me up for no reason and everyone laughs. My trousers are all ripped and my knee is bleeding. But I don't say anything: that would make it worse. I just limp away.

Charlie goes to kick the ball, still laughing, but before his foot can connect, a furious little figure appears. She puffs out her cheeks and blows at the football, looking exactly like a cherub in one of those old-style maps – a really MAD cherub…

The ball zooms across the playground like a feather in a hurricane. Charlie totally misses the kick and falls over. I'm so stunned I forget all about

the blood trickling down my knee. Charlie looks stunned too. He just sits there with his mouth hanging open, wondering what happened.

When the bell rings for home time, I don't rush out of the school gates with the other kids. What is there to rush home for? A pathetic excuse for a party. A home that is just one step up from a hippie camp site, and which is going to be packed into boxes any day now. Then Mum and I will be back in a big white van, with all our belongings crashing around like World War Two, while we try to find the right exit on yet another strange roundabout. We've been going round in circles ever since Dad left, and I'm just so tired.

I trudge slowly down the school corridor. But I think I must have caught Lilac Peabody's alien Special Powers. An electric flash of excitement goes through me a split second before I hear the noise.

It's actually more of a ruckus. A cheerful happy carnival ruckus.

Loud jolly oompa oompa music. Cheering and laughter. And my name. People are calling my name! I start to run. My heart is bumping in my chest.

On the other side of the school gates is a brightly painted circus truck, with BRIGHT'S CIRCUS on the side in huge rainbow-coloured letters. Clowns, jugglers, and acrobats in bright gaudy costumes are piled inside.

Bella is waving madly. "Sam, quickly! Come over here!"

"What's going on?" I ask in a dazed voice. I feel as if I'm dreaming.

"It's my birthday surprise!" she beams. "They let me call Dad from the school office at lunch time. He loves anything like this. Look!"

She points to the big banner hanging from the side of the truck.

"HAPPY BIRTHDAY SAM," I read aloud.

Two girl acrobats are pulling faces at me from inside the truck. They look exactly like taller, more confident versions of Bella.

"They're my cousins," she explains.

Shy mousy Bella Bright comes from a circus family. I can't believe it!

"Excuse me," I say suddenly. "I just have to talk to someone."

She's here. Of course she's here. And suddenly I'm so over the moon! I don't give a hoot if people do see me talking to a glow-in-the-dark alien who doesn't actually exist.

"You did it, Peebs!" I tell her. "You used your Special Powers!"

Her eyes are sparkling. She's so happy for me. But she has to set the record straight. "No, Sam," she says firmly. "You did!"

4.
Home Sweet Home

I can hear Mum's voice. I push my way through the crowd and find her talking to a man with a huge moustache and a top hat.

"This must be Sam Sparks," he booms in a

heavy foreign accent. "I can tell. You've got your mother's eyes."

It's Bella's dad: the circus ringmaster who likes to give birthday surprises to total strangers.

"Hey Sparkster!" Mum beams. "I see you've made some new friends."

She doesn't seem at all surprised to find herself mixing with circus folk. My mum's cool like that.

"Sorry I had to go out so early this morning," she says in my ear. "I had to organise your special birthday surprise. I'll tell you about that later."

I tell her it's fine, which by this time it is. But I'm fairly sure Mum's "surprise" can't top being met out of school by my own personal birthday circus!

Mum and I climb into the front of the truck with Bella and her dad.

Bella's dad picks up a megaphone and booms out of the window to the other kids. "Go home and tell your parents there's a free circus performance in the park at six o'clock to celebrate Sam Sparks's birthday. You're ALL invited!"

Everyone claps and cheers, except for Honey Hope, who just goes stumping off like the bad fairy in a pantomime.

I feel like some hotshot celebrity, driving through the streets in the big painted circus truck, with everyone staring and waving. When we reach the park behind our house I'm amazed to see they've already set up the Big Top.

Kids start to turn up long before it's time for the performance. The first one to arrive is Charlie. He walks right up to me, sticks out his hand and apologises for tripping me up. "I do these mad things," he says. "I don't even know why sometimes."

"No problem," I tell him. "Everyone does mad things."

He glances round to make sure no one is listening. "It was spooky the way that ball just

moved by itself," he says in a low voice.

"Yeah, it was," I grin.

At last Bella leads me and Mum to our VIP seats in the front row.

You wouldn't think a small family circus could be that special, but it's the best, most brilliant circus performance I have ever seen. The trapeze artists are fantastic. The clowns are cool too. They drive into the ring in one of those crazy cars that eventually ends up exploding into about a zillion tiny pieces. Charlie laughs so much he's almost sick.

At the end, all the circus performers run back in to take a bow, and everyone turns to me and sings *Happy Birthday* and I feel myself go as red as a beetroot.

Afterwards there's a birthday tea in the circus tent. What with the food my mum bought and the fabulous goodies contributed by Bella's family, there's so much food Charlie says he won't need to eat again for a month!

Mum gives me my presents, including the sports strip I've been hinting about for weeks and a cool Game Boy from my Auntie Jasmine, which I'd NO idea she was planning to get.

"Thanks, Mum," I tell her.

At that moment two clowns run in, wheeling a trolley with the most enormous cake I have ever seen on it. On top are ten lighted candles.

Bella's dad says I have to blow them all out in one go.

"It won't explode will it?" I ask nervously.

Bella giggles. "No dumbo. It's a special Italian chocolate cake my great-grandmother makes for people's birthdays, so you've got to try some even if your buttons are popping off."

She looks like a different person out of school. Almost as cheeky and confident as her cousins.

"Thanks, Bella," I tell her. "This is the best birthday I've ever had."

Her face lights up. "Really?"

By this time everyone's yelling, "Make a wish! Make a wish!" I try to think what to wish for, but it seems like Lilac Peabody's got all the bases covered, plus I've never been so happy in my life, so I shut my eyes and make a wish for Bella. I wish she could be as happy as she was before she and Honey broke friends.

At last the party is over.

The circus people start to take down the Big Top and Mum and I go home. We walk up our garden path in the dusk and let ourselves back into our house.

That's when I remember that my birthday happiness can't last. We'll be moving to London any day now.

But I'm not sad about giving my birthday wish away to Bella. After all those weeks and months of the Honey Hope treatment, she deserves a break.

I go and brush my teeth and get into bed. Mum comes in. She's got a mischievous sparkle in her eyes.

"Hey, Sparkster," she says. "I've saved your biggest present till last."

"Excellent," I say greedily. "Hand it over!"

I wait for her to produce a huge parcel, but she just gives me an envelope, a big posh one with a dark-blue tissue-paper lining. On the front it says: SAM SPARKS. OFFICIAL DOCUMENTS.

I rip it open and take out a pile of papers, full of boring grown-up words that I can't begin to understand.

"What is it?" I ask, bewildered.

"The deeds to our house," she beams. "I bought it. We'll never have to move again if you don't want to. Well, not for years and years. I went to sign the papers this morning at the solicitor's."

"I thought we were moving to London!" I gasp.

"London?" says Mum. "No way!"

It takes about twenty seconds to sort out our little misunderstanding.

I'd got it all wrong. Mum had let Auntie Jasmine in on the big house-buying secret. My aunt knew our place needed a lot of work, so she offered to drive up to help us decorate. I'd overheard Mum giving her directions!

"You are pleased aren't you, Sam?" Mum asks anxiously.

I just throw my arms around her and I hug my mum so hard she has to beg for mercy.

An hour or so later, I'm drifting off to sleep, when there's a familiar *fitzz*! Lilac is there, sitting cross-legged on my bed in a halo of honey-gold light.

"Hi Sam," she says. "How does it feel to make things happen?"

"Good," I tell her drowsily. "Amazing actually."

I sit up in the dark. We just look at each other and I feel my new Special Powers kick in. Lilac Peabody has come to say goodbye.

"Who are you, Peebs? I mean really," I whisper. "You're not a fairy are you?"

She pulls a mad face. "Please! With this waistline?"

We both giggle.

"Extraterrestrial Busybody, Cosmic Beach-comber, Intergalactic Party Planner, Positive Thinker — what else is on your passport?" I ask her.

"Friend," she says softly. "Your glow-in-the-dark alien friend."

"But how did you *know*?" I ask. "How could you know what would happen?"

Lilac Peabody gives me her secretive smile.

"Confidential info, right?" I sigh.

I'm not sure if her species is into hugging, or whether I'll just embarrass us both, so we bump cheeks rather awkwardly. I get about a billion tiny electric shocks, but I don't care.

Lilac Peabody may not be real in the usual sense, but as a friend, she's just the best. If I'm ever in trouble again, she'll be there for me. But for the time being I've got everything I need, and more.

Lilac doesn't leave straight away. She sits beside me, filling my room with her soft golden glow, humming dreamily.

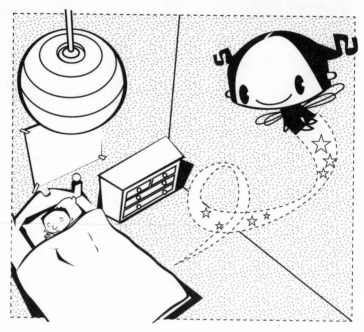

As I float away into a deep peaceful sleep, I recognise the tune: a weird extraterrestrial version of *Home Sweet Home*.

PERTH AND KINROSS LIBRARIES

Lilac Peabody

and Bella Bright

ANNIE DALTON
Illustrated by Griff

Lilac Peabody is a friend to ALL children who need her.

Bella Bright could do with a friend right now.
Find out what happens when Lilac Peabody, the
Extraterrestrial Busybody, Cosmic Beachcomber,
Intergalactic Party Planner and Positive Thinker,
flies into Bella's life…

ISBN 0 00 713772 9

An imprint of HarperCollins*Publishers*

www.roaringgoodreads.co.uk

MR SKIP

★ MICHAEL MORPURGO

ILLUSTRATED BY GRIFF

When Jackie finds a broken garden gnome in a rubbish skip, she is determined to make him as good as new. In return, Mister Skip makes Jackie's wishes come true… almost! A fairy-tale for today from a master storyteller.

ISBN 0 00 713474 6

ROARING GOOD READS

Collins

An imprint of HarperCollins*Publishers*

www.roaringgoodreads.co.uk

Jean Ure

Illustrated by Karen Donnelly

For the first ten years of her life, Daisy lives in the Foundling Hospital with lots of other orphans. But on her tenth birthday she goes to work at the Dobell Academy for young ladies. There she watches, listens, learns and dreams. A 'rags-to-riches' story with a difference, where dreams really can come true!

ISBN 0 00 713369 3

An imprint of HarperCollins*Publishers*

www.roaringgoodreads.co.uk

Other exciting titles available in the Roaring Good Reads series:

Short, lively stories, with illustrations on every page, for children just starting to read by themselves

Morris the Mouse Hunter *Vivian French*
Morris and the Cat Flap *Vivian French*
The Littlest Dragon *Margaret Ryan*

For confident readers, with short chapters and illustrations throughout

Daisy May *Jean Ure*
Dazzling Danny *Jean Ure*
Down with the Dirty Danes *Gillian Cross*
The Gargling Gorilla *Margaret Mahy*
King Henry VIII's Shoes *Karen Wallace*
Lilac Peabody and Sam Sparks *Annie Dalton*
Mr Skip *Michael Morpurgo*
Spider McDrew *Alan Durant*
Witch-in-Training: Flying Lessons *Maeve Friel*
Witch-in-Training: Spelling Trouble *Maeve Friel*
Witch-in-Training: Charming or What? *Maeve Friel*
Witch-in-Training: Brewing Up *Maeve Friel*
The Witch's Tears *Jenny Nimmo*

A longer novel for confident readers

Elephant Child *Mary Ellis*